TIME SLIDE

Marie Godley

Raider Publishing International

New York   London   Cape Town

© 2010 Marie Godley

All rights reserved. No part of this book may be reproduced stored in a retrieval system or transmitted in any form by any means with out the prior written permission of the publisher, except by a reviewer who may quote brief passages in a review to be printed in a newspaper, magazine or journal.

First Printing

The views, content and descriptions in this book do not represent the views of Raider Publishing International. Some of the content may be offensive to some readers and they are to be advised. Objections to the content in this book should be directed towards the author and owner of the intellectual property rights as registered with their local government.

All characters portrayed in this book are fictitious and any resemblance to persons living or dead is purely coincidental.

ISBN: 978-1-61667-093-1

Published By Raider Publishing International
www.RaiderPublishing.com
New York London Cape Town
Printed in the United States of America and the United Kingdom

TIME SLIDE

Marie Godley

1
Jerry & Sammy

"I'M THE LUCKIEST CHILD ALIVE. I TRAVEL THROUGH TIME. *Today Ancient Egypt, tomorrow Greece; I hold their possessions in my hands; see into their worlds. I study their culture; learn from them... and wonder what it would be like to actually meet them!*"

That's how Jerry started the entry in his journal for that day.

Jerry Slade, a tall thin youth with curly hair and dark blue eyes, lived with his sister in Charforth. Their parents were archaeologists who travelled the world from one site to another before returning home.

Sometimes, during the school holidays, the children were allowed to accompany David and Christine on their digs. Jerry's sister, Sammy, was only ten, a couple of years younger than he, so it was Jerry who was dying to follow in his parent's footsteps. History was in his blood and, needless to say, his favourite subject at school. If Jerry wasn't studying actual artefacts, he was reading about different civilisations in books or on the Internet.

Sammy was still undecided. Becoming a relic hunter would be cool but she hadn't given up all hope of finding her way into an enchanted land full of unicorns. Jerry was always teasing her that she didn't make sense. She was the top student in her martial art class, who didn't like violence. She wanted to be a relic hunter but didn't like insects and she still loved unicorns and fairies.

She spent ages tying her long hair in different styles, making sure she had the right look for every occasion from relic hunting and fighting off ninjas to meeting the king of the unicorns. She believed in being prepared.

Sammy didn't take any notice of Jerry's teasing. She thought he was narrow minded, only caring about historical things and that he needed a little more imagination in his life. Together, however, they made a good team and found they relied on each other a lot when their parents were away and they were left in the charge of their grandparents.

Their grandparents, Audrey and Bob, were great. They always had time to listen to them and made things fun but stuck to the rules. They encouraged them to try new things besides history, although they knew that with both parents being archaeologists they couldn't get away from it.

You only had to look around David and Christine's home. The walls had displays of ancient masks made of gold from Greece and a clay mask depicting the giant Humbaba from Mesopotamia. The cupboards were full of pottery; some shards and some complete objects. These ranged from Romans to Victorian. Obviously most of the finds went to museums but there was usually some to fill up all the nooks and crannies in the house and Jerry and Sammy were beginning to build up quite a collection of their own.

Although the children got on well with Audrey and Bob and had each other, they still missed their parents when they were away and were happy when they returned. Sometimes though, Sammy said it took longer for her parents to return to 'the present' than it did to return home.

* * *

IT USUALLY TOOK DAVID A COUPLE OF DAYS BEFORE HE fully noticed the children and talked about them and not the latest finds. However, both children loved their parents and knew they were loved in return. They were also proud of their achievements and it was this that inspired their own interest in history. They knew that even if they chose a different career the example that their parents set would mean that they would commit all their effort into making it a success.

There was a knock at Jerry's door. He put aside his journal to answer it. Audrey was there.

"Tea is ready. Your mum and dad said they'd ring at 5.30," she reminded him.

"Thanks, Grandma, I'll be straight down." Jerry smiled at her before closing his door. Once he'd put his journal safely in his cluttered drawer he went down to join the others.

David and Christine would be home in two days. The dig in Bath had finished earlier than expected and the local archaeologists were going to file the paperwork.

"What do you think they wanted to talk about?" asked Sammy.

"I don't know, do I?" answered Jerry. "They said it had to do with the summer holidays but they didn't tell me any more than you, did they?"

He was getting slightly annoyed with Sammy's insistence that being older he would know more. They'd listened to the same phone call. Jerry just hoped his parents weren't leaving them to go on another dig already. The summer holidays were only eight weeks away.

2

Plans for the Summer

DAVID AND CHRISTINE SLADE ARRIVED THROUGH the front door and dumped their bulging bags on the polished wooden floor of the hallway. It had been an arduous three-hour drive and they were glad to be home. Suddenly, with the only warning being a squeal, they found themselves enveloped in a bear hug as Sammy hurled herself at them, closely followed by Jerry, trying to act more grown up but just as delighted to have them home.

"How are you? How was the dig? Did you find anything good?" The children's questions tumbled out thick and fast without their pausing for breath.

"Let us get in and have a cup of tea," laughed their mum.

Christine relaxed on the sofa with her drink and Sammy snuggled up against her, enjoying the feel of her mum's soft curly hair on her cheek. Their tea finished and the children's questions exhausted, they spoke to Jerry and Sammy about a more serious matter.

"We have been invited by the University of Beijing to take part in a dig in the summer," announced David.

The news was met by a deafening silence.

"You mean you're leaving again so soon?" said Jerry, a troubled look on his face.

"No, Sweetheart," interjected Christine quickly. "You two can come along. We are working with some archaeological students from the university with one of their professors. They are happy for you to join us and help out. We explained we couldn't take part unless you were able to come as well."

"Wow! That's so cool!" exclaimed Sammy.

"What are we going to excavate?" asked Jerry.

Sammy rolled her eyes. "Summer in China and all you can think about is what we are going to dig up," she teased.

Jerry threw a cushion at her.

David and Christine told them they were going to look at the ruins of Xanadu, the summer palace of Kublai Khan, a little way outside the Great Wall of China. It was important for the students to undertake a real dig and record and document it. Because it had been excavated already there wasn't likely to be anything new or unusual uncovered on the site so the Slades had been invited along as guest archaeologists.

"The Chinese are rightly protective of their history and this is a really good opportunity for us to take part in an official dig. If we can forge a good relationship whilst we assist the university it may open the door for cooperation on further digs," David pointed out.

Jerry spent the next hour in his bedroom doing research on the Internet.

David had shut himself away too; he was in his study checking on his post and messages.

Sammy and her mum chatted whilst they unpacked and started dinner. "Will we have time for any sight seeing?" Sammy asked when she had finished telling her mum all that had happened while they had been away.

"I'm not sure about the exact dates or our schedule yet, Honey. We needed to speak to you and Jerry before we arranged anything but I expect we will have to spend a couple of days in Beijing before we go out to the dig site. There will probably be papers that need filling in and we've got to meet one of the students who is going to act as our interpreter during our stay. I hope we can squeeze in a couple of trips too. Can you imagine going to China and not seeing anything of its history?" answered Christine, a playful smile beginning to tug at the corner of her mouth.

"Not good," said Sammy. "Especially for archaeologists," then promptly fell about laughing.

David entered their large, homely kitchen to find Sammy and her mum still laughing. However much he loved his work it was always good to come home to scenes like this. He would ring Audrey and Bob later. They had vanished, as usual, the minute he and Christine had arrived home to give the family time alone, despite being told they didn't have to. He knew he was lucky to be able to rely on them so much.

* * *

"A TRIP TO CHINA! WHAT ORIENTAL TREASURE MIGHT *I uncover? A jade statue or maybe a Mongolian horse bit.*" For once Jerry's imagination was running away with him, albeit about artefacts as he wrote in his journal.

Jerry's writing was interrupted by Sammy as she came crashing through his door, without knocking - a sure sign she was excited; she was usually really good about respecting his privacy. Jerry quickly shut his book and scowled at her but before he could say anything she apologised.

"I'm sorry. I forgot to knock. What have you got there?"

"It's my journal," he admitted and waited for her next remark with trepidation.

"Cool! I didn't know you kept a journal. Why do you keep it secret? What do you write about?" Sammy couldn't help asking questions.

As Jerry had expected her to tease him he found himself off guard and answering her.

"I write about whatever I want to; might be stuff we've found or things that are happening. I keep it secret so nobody is tempted to read it. That way I can write what I like without worrying even if it is personal."

He looked at Sammy and could see she was giving some serious thought to this.

"Do you think I could keep a journal?" she finally asked.

"I don't see why not. It's up to you, isn't it?" Jerry said.

He put his journal in his drawer and smiled at her, knowing he didn't have to ask her to keep his secret.

3
A Meeting of Two Cultures

The Slades had waited a long time at the airport and had occupied themselves by wandering around the shops. Now they were finally aboard the plane and were starting to taxi down the runway. Sammy squeezed Jerry's hand for reassurance. She hadn't made up her mind about flying either. Once they were airborne Jerry rummaged around in his rucksack, checked his parents weren't watching and handed Sammy a little package. She unwrapped it and found a stripy pink and yellow notebook with a pen to match.

"Just in case," said Jerry in answer to Sammy's quizzical look.

"Oh! A journal," whispered Sammy. "Thank you."

* * *

TEN HOURS LATER THE PLANE LANDED AND THE TRAVEL weary family was able to stretch their cramped muscles. They collected their luggage from the slow moving carousel and left the airport. Luckily, a car was waiting to take them to their hotel.

The sights and sounds of Beijing were completely different to what the children were used to. There were people and vehicles everywhere, jostling for position in the streets. Traffic rumbled past their car; scooters weaved in and out, and people seemed to just step off the pavement. Sammy found herself covering her eyes until Jerry poked her. A man wobbled past on a bike, which was piled as high as his head with boxes. As they neared a market area their senses were overpowered by colours and smells. The stalls seemed to be selling everything imaginable in all colours of the rainbow, whilst various foods were being cooked in the open. The children were horrified to see insects being fried and sold on sticks. Jerry and Sammy turned away from the window until they'd passed the market; quite sure the driver was taking the 'scenic' route on purpose probably for the benefit of their parents to show them the sights.

"Here we are," said David.

The children dared to look out of the window and were quite disappointed to see a modern hotel. They could have been back in England.

Once they were in their room their disappointment vanished as they discovered they had a suite. There was plenty of room with a sofa, table and chairs, a computer desk and a room each, off the living area. After running from room to room, exploring, they looked out of the windows. One gave them a view of the still bustling street whilst on the opposite side the view was far more tranquil. The window overlooked the small garden that belonged to the hotel.

There was a gravel area with a sturdy wooden bench, a water feature and lots of foliage in varying shades of green interspersed with flowers. In contrast to the street the garden looked frozen but when you looked closely there was gentle movement. The plants swayed in the breeze, the water trickled out of the end of the bamboo pole, which then shot up to catch the next stream of water. Sammy sensed it was a peaceful place and couldn't wait to visit it. However the next place that needed visiting was the museum where they were to meet their interpreter and the minister of culture.

4
Centuries of History

ALAN LEE SPOKE EXCELLENT ENGLISH AND WAS VERY friendly. Jerry and Sammy breathed a sigh of relief. They'd imagined that he would be a stuffy, middle-aged man, not a lively youngster. He took them inside and introduced everyone to Mr. Wu, the minister of culture. Mr. Wu was a dignified man in an elegant suit, obviously very proud of his position but very welcoming, nonetheless.

As David and Christine had to go and fill in some paperwork, Mr. Wu suggested that the children stay downstairs and look around the exhibits.

Sammy was grateful to be missing the paperwork; she could get bored easily. Jerry had wished to go with them. He wanted to learn everything to do with being an archaeologist. However he changed his mind once he saw the extent of the exhibits.

The children started off together but as usual, drifted apart. Jerry liked to read every notice in every case (Luckily they were translated into English as well). Sammy preferred to look at all the objects and read the titles, until she discovered something that took her fancy. Then she would be there for ages!

Jerry found the museum fascinating. His brain soaked up as much information as possible like a sponge. He searched for Sammy. She was a little way over and, for once, she was standing still.

Sammy was reading about an area that was now part of Beijing but could be traced back to as far as early man. Originally it was marshland for early man to live off. Through the centuries various wealthy merchants and rulers built palaces and cities changing the landscape forever until its final change: the building of the Forbidden City and the naming of Beijing as the capital in the 15th century. The only change in modern times had been its expansion and the addition of skyscrapers.

The Forbidden City was a palace museum now. Sammy had seen photos of it and had hoped to be able to visit it during their trip. She beckoned Jerry over and he too got lost in the history of the area.

Sammy had noticed a separate notice board titled 'Mystery' with a painting of a young lady on it. The lady was pretty, dressed in fine silk with an exquisite gold and jade hair slide holding back her upswept hair. Her name was Lotus and she had been the daughter of a wealthy merchant. They had lived in a pavilion in the city of Zhongdu in the Jin dynasty. Lotus had disappeared from her home one night and despite the best efforts of her father and his servants, as well as some of the guards from the gatehouse, no trace was ever found of her.

There were many theories. Some say she left unnoticed and fled, some she fell into the moat. The other unlikely theory was that she had been kidnapped to cause a conflict. No evidence was uncovered and over time Lotus was all but forgotten by everyone except her family who bequeathed her painting to the museum. She was being kept 'alive' through the exhibit.

Sammy stared at the painting and the strangest sensation came over her. She felt hot and dizzy. The room began to blur and she could have sworn she saw Lotus in front of her, in the flesh. Then nothing!

Startled, she turned to find Jerry shaking her arm. "Wake up. Mum and Dad are coming.

* * *

"THE MUSEUM WAS SO COOL. MUM AND DAD HAVE *to wait for a couple of days for all the paperwork so we're going sight seeing tomorrow."*
"I felt weird in the museum today. I thought I saw Lotus. I guess I must have been dreaming."

Sammy closed her journal. It was good to be able to write things down. She was grateful to Jerry for being so thoughtful as to get her a journal of her own. Now she must go to sleep. It had been a long day and she was ready to test out her pillow.

5
Amazing Sights

THE SLADES COULD HARDLY CONTAIN THEIR EXCITEMENT and were finding it hard to sit still. They were going to Xian to see the Terracotta warriors. Alan arrived in a large, black car to pick them up. He was acting as their unofficial tour guide. With him was his friend, Kim. He was going to be with them for most of the summer too. Although he wasn't an archaeological student he was of Mongolian descent and had family amongst the nomadic tribe which still visited the site of the dig.

As he was planning to visit his family anyway, Alan and Professor Cho had invited him to join them because he, too, spoke English and it would help to have a spare interpreter along. Jerry and Sammy took to Kim immediately. He was just as friendly as Alan and they could see that they were good friends.

Alan informed David and Christine that Professor Cho was leaving for the dig site that morning. There was some paperwork to be finalised and picked up from Mr. Wu and then they could follow on the next day.

It was a long journey to Xian. Alan and Kim were happy to tell the family all about themselves. Alan had lived in London for a year with his family, which explained his excellent English. His father had been transferred there on business and still visited once a year.

It was essential that Kim spoke good English, too. He was studying law at university. His parents had decided to give up the nomadic Mongolian life when Kim was born but his grandmother and uncle still continued to live in the traditional way, moving their yurts (portable houses) in the summer to the best grazing places. It was this family that Kim was planning to visit and he was hoping that Jerry and Sammy might be lucky enough to witness the festival of Nadam. The festival takes place every summer and includes many sporting events, the most famous being a horse race in which children as young as five enter.

Once inside the underground complex at Xian, the Slades were overcome at the spectacle that was before them. Of course they had seen photos but nothing prepared them for the sight that met them. There were row upon row of terracotta figures as far as the eye could see. David and Christine started asking all sorts of questions about the excavation so, before the children got restless, Kim took them off to look around.

They entered pit two, expecting and anticipating more soldiers. They weren't disappointed but what was even more exciting was the display of horses with chariots and archers kneeling, ready to fire their arrows. Despite the fact there were other tourists around, the sight and atmosphere was so intense that they faded into the background and Jerry felt as if he was the only person there. He took in all the different styles of uniform, weapons and hair.

Kim told him that these differences signified what rank the men were. Jerry saw them in his mind's eye as individuals in the great army, sent to protect the first Emperor, Qin Shi Huangdi.

Sammy had been absorbed in the figures too. Suddenly, she went hot and dizzy. The soldiers became a blur then returned into focus; but this time they weren't a dusty stone colour, they were brightly coloured with paint.

"They're all different colours," she exclaimed.

Everything went blank. She turned to Jerry to find him staring at her strangely.

"What did you say?" asked Jerry.

"I saw soldiers in bright colours," said Sammy.

"The soldiers were originally painted," said Kim looking confused.

"Did you read about that?" asked Jerry, thinking she was just giving them some information.

"No, I saw them," replied Sammy, although with slightly less conviction.

"You can't have," persisted Jerry. "You must have been imagining it. Maybe jet lag is catching up with you."

Neither Sammy nor Jerry mentioned it again and apart from enthusing about their visit, Sammy was quiet on the way back.

Once they reached their hotel room both children shut themselves away in their bedrooms. Jerry started writing in his journal straight away.

"I'd stepped back in time. I was amongst the warriors, seeing the expressions on their faces as they lined up. Of course, it helps that all the soldiers are individuals. Even the horses seemed different though, standing tall and looking ready to pull the chariots. I know they're of stone but they represent a real army and the emperor believed he'd need them after death. Sammy said she saw the soldiers brightly coloured and Kim said they had been painted originally. Jet lag or picturing what they looked like probably. What an awesome day!"

Sammy was still thoughtful. Twice now she'd had the same sensation followed by a strange vision. It had lasted only a moment but it felt so real. She decided to write it into her journal to see if putting it down on paper would help her.

"Twice now, I've seen things from the past come alive. There seems to be no explanation and it's over so quickly. Am I imagining it, Should I tell Mum and Dad? I don't think so. What would I say. I don't think I'll tell Jerry about

the museum either. Maybe he's right and its jet lag. Anyway we should be off tomorrow. I can't wait to get to the dig."

6

Arriving in Xanadu

WITH THE LAST NIGHT IN A HOTEL FOR A WHILE BEHIND them and a lengthy journey in front of them, the Slades were impatient to start. One last check that they had everything, especially the important paperwork that Mr. Wu had given them that morning, and they were finally underway. Alan and Kim were travelling with them and were once again happy to point out anything interesting along the way. They passed through the Great Wall on the main road. It seemed strange to Sammy to be driven through it. She'd always pictured it as one wall. Alan explained that originally it was a series of walls that were eventually joined to make one wall under the Qin dynasty and rebuilt again during the Ming dynasty. Throughout its history, some parts were still made of mud and some sections were better guarded depending on who commanded the garrison left to defend it.

The motion of the car caused Sammy to drift off to sleep as it began the drive through the arid landscape. Jerry took the opportunity to talk to Kim about the Mongols. So much was made about the history of the Mongol raids on China but there wasn't much information about the people themselves or their traditions. Kim told him of the calligraphers and scholars, the advances in medical science and astronomy that many people didn't know about. He said that he would be able to show them the yurts when they went to visit his family.

Jerry was less troubled now that he had satisfied himself that he had filled in the gaps in his sketchy research and knew more about Mongol history. He liked to have a thorough knowledge of anything that interested him. He was sure to learn more when he met Kim's relatives and was able to witness their way of life first hand.

When Sammy woke up it was to find that the landscape was changing and that the sandy expanses were giving way to green pastures. Kim said they were getting to the region known as Xanadu. The area was more fertile because of the close proximity to the Yellow River. It was for this reason that the Mongolians moved their animals there in the summer.

"That is also why the emperor built his summer palace here; to escape from the heat in the city," finished Alan.

The car passed the outer area of Xanadu. It was mainly pasture with grass-covered mounds and the odd pile of rubble. They were heading nearer to the middle of the palace complex. Rows of tents came into view as the driver stopped the car.

Professor Cho, a small but charismatic looking man, stopped work and came over and greeted everybody. Alan explained that the students were only going to work for another hour so Professor Cho thought that the Slades would like to unpack and freshen up first. Then he would take them round the dig whilst the students were changing. Dinner would be in the marquee at 7pm.

David and Christine had the last but one tent next to Alan and Kim. Jerry and Sammy were to share a tent on the end. They didn't like this idea and pulled faces at each other until they entered their tent to find two bedroom areas separated by a zipped screen and enough space for them to sit together as well. Their faces wore big grins; they had the most 'upmarket' tent on the whole site, except for the dining marquee of course. They gleefully set to work unpacking their bags.

* * *

JERRY AND SAMMY WANDERED AROUND THE TENT CITY that had sprung up. Jerry smiled to think of the contrast to the original palace. Professor Cho showed them where they were excavating the palace rooms. David and Christine were going to help here and on one of the corner towers. The children assumed they would be working with their parents but when they heard about the temple area with gardens and a workshop they asked Professor Cho if it would be possible for them to help there. They held their breath whilst Alan translated.

"Professor Cho says there is only one student working over there and is worried about you being on your own," said Alan.

Jerry and Sammy were disappointed but did their best not to show it. They were visitors after all and only children at that.

"Can I help?" enquired Kim. "I know I'm not an archaeologist but if I accompanied the children I could translate for them. Would that work?"

Professor Cho called the student over. Her name was Jia-Li and despite the fact that she had been in the 'finds' tent she looked fresh and unaffected by the heat. After a rapid discussion in Chinese she turned and smiled at the children.

"Jia-Li would be happy for you to join her. She will welcome the company for as long as you want. She will wait for you in the morning and take you over so you can find a good spot to excavate."

"Thank you," said the children.

Sammy thought Jia-Li was very pretty with her dark hair and smooth complexion and she seemed very kind. This was reinforced by her bright smile and willingness to have the children share her excavation site.

Jerry and Sammy scrambled into their tent, full of excitement. They could hardly contain themselves. Their first visit to China and they were going to be allowed to work on their own. They didn't think they would get any sleep that night, but within an hour they were snoring gently.

7
Meeting Mongolians

LIFE QUICKLY SETTLED DOWN INTO A ROUTINE. DAVID and Christine worked in the main areas of the palace, wherever they were needed whilst Jerry and Sammy accompanied Jia-Li to the temple area. Kim followed on almost immediately, in case they needed anything. Jia-Li was very helpful to the children and was happy to stop and offer advice. However, she knew how important it was to gain experience so she left them alone as much as possible. Kim talked to the children or Jia-Li without disturbing them and tried his hand at excavating as well. He said it was fun but he wouldn't give up his dream of becoming a lawyer. Between them they had found some pottery fragments and marble shards, probably from temple or garden statues. Everything was documented and photographed carefully and the children were pleased when Jia-Li told Professor Cho that they were very professional.

It was hard to believe that they had been there for a couple of weeks already. Most of the students were going back to Beijing for the weekend with the professor to get more supplies and to deposit any catalogued finds back at the museum. Although the trips back were frantic the professor found it easier to give the students a break and it gave him the opportunity to take some of the finds off the site to the safety of the museum without having to wait until the end of the dig.

Kim invited Alan and the Slades to stay behind and visit his family with him, as he was going to the Festival of Nadam and his family had expressed an interest in meeting his friends.

On the pastures the next morning there was a sense of bubbling anticipation. Even from the dig site you could make out buildings and people. When they got closer the buildings turned out to be many yurts erected overnight by the now milling crowds, turning the small nomadic camp into a busy sprawling town. Everywhere you looked there were people in bright coloured silks mixed in with lots of horses of varying shades from chestnut to pale dun. Different areas had been set aside so people could practise sports like archery and wrestling. Food and drink were also being prepared and laid out while hand-made crafts were arranged on tables or blankets. The scene was completed by the array of people sitting outside their yurts, talking and laughing. Outside one yurt, Kim was warmly greeted by a man, obviously his uncle, whilst a small girl threw herself against him and wrapped her arms around his knee. Kim bent down to pick her up, tossed her into the air causing her plaits to curve upwards onto her head, and amidst her delighted giggles turned to introduce everybody. Alan had met Kim's uncle, Quan once before and was quickly introduced to Poppy so he could distract her. Poppy was a livewire and although not spoilt, loved to be near people and enjoyed involving everyone in her games. Alan was soon busy with Poppy so Quan ushered the Slades inside the yurt before Poppy could seize them too.

Kim's grandma was sitting on a low, wooden bench, which was carved all along the front. She was an impressive sight. Her black hair, now streaked with grey, was parted down the middle and plaited with small beads at the end. Her skin was wrinkled with age and tanned from her outdoor existence but she was wise and had a youthful twinkle in her eyes.

Quan and Grandma talked to the Slades about their history and way of life, but they were equally interested in all the Slades did. Jerry and Sammy were not treated as little kids and were happy to be included in the grown-up's conversation.

Poppy arrived through the doorway and broke the thread of the conversation, which gave Jerry a chance to look around at the yurt. It was a series of trellis-like walls with a covering over them, forming a waterproof barrier and a roof. It was plain to see how it could be moved around easily.

"Tell me a story, Grandma," said Poppy, her long, dark lashes framing her eyes as she gave her grandma her most adoring look in the hope of getting her own way.

"It's the only time she sits still," smiled Quan.

"Not now," said Grandma giving Poppy a hug. "The races are about to start. If you are good I will tell you of the beautiful runaway later.

Poppy clapped her hands at this, promising to be good. Sammy smiled at her enthusiasm and didn't object when Poppy grabbed her hand to take her outside. Grandma looked at Sammy for a minute and then said, "You will enjoy that story." Nothing more and no explanations. Sammy was confused, was she saying Sammy was childish?

The horse race was very exciting. Kids everywhere were jumping onto their horses and galloping off across the open grassland, their scarves and tassels billowing behind them. They went so far so fast that they ended up as colourful blurs on the horizon. Alan and the Slades watched all the events, tried a few activities and sampled the food. The wonderful smells had been making their tummies rumble!

After the meal everyone gathered around a crackling fire. It wasn't really needed for warmth but it set the scene for the storytellers. They spoke thanks for the land, the protection of their flocks and their way of life. They told how their tribe dated back centuries and was known as The Swan Tribe because they cared for the swans on the lake, which were regarded as 'Birds of God'.

Poppy was snuggled on Sammy's lap and, as her father had said, had sat quietly listening to everyone but her eyes kept searching out her grandma to see if she was going to speak next.

Grandma started her narration and Sammy sat as enthralled as Poppy. She told of a beautiful Chinese girl who fell in love with a young man from their tribe, how they eventually ran away together and lived happily until the end of their lives. It made Sammy think of Lotus, probably because of the fact they were both pretty Chinese girls. Some of the others gathered around the fire seemed to be getting restless.

"Some feel this is nothing but a fairy tale," whispered Kim. "But Grandma firmly believes that it is our history and Poppy hangs on to her every word. I can see her telling this story to other children when she is Grandma's age."

When it came time for the visitors to return to their camp they found themselves treated as one of the family with handshakes and hugs. Poppy didn't want to let Sammy go, hanging on tightly whilst Quan tried to extract Sammy from her grip. Kim had to promise he would bring them back for another weekend before she would let go.

Grandma hugged Sammy then kept her close for a minute as she said, "You are a very spiritual person; in tune with nature and sensitive to people. That's a special quality."

Sammy wasn't sure what to say, or even if it meant anything. Maybe Grandma was just being nice.

Jerry was full of his visit all the way back to camp, going on about all the things he had tried out and learnt.

After such an interesting day there was silence in camp the minute everybody got into bed (except for the occasional snore!).

8
A Discovery

JERRY AND SAMMY TOOK ADVANTAGE OF THE PEACE in camp the next morning to update their journals. In the last couple of weeks the entries had only been about the finds or the dig itself.

"*I travelled through time yesterday,*" Jerry wrote, "*or so it seemed when I stepped into the Mongolian yurt. They are constructed practically the same as they have been for centuries although in the past they were covered in felt. Talking to Quan he told me that some modern Mongolians build themselves yurt like structures from mud to live in and those families that have decided to live in one place and even have appliances in theirs. Although he doesn't, the yurt we saw yesterday is a traditional travelling one. They have a larger one for use in winter, which gives better protection from the weather and more room to enable them to make their crafts. They were lovely people and I can picture all that Kim had told me more clearly having met them. I wish I could ride a horse as well as some of those youngsters!*"

Sammy was equally eager to write down her feelings about the Mongolians.

"*What a lovely family Kim has! Poppy was such fun but I'm not sure what to make of Grandma; apparently everyone calls her that. She said some strange things to me about being in tune with nature and she told a story she said I would enjoy about a Chinese girl who ran away with a man from their tribe. I thought about Lotus after she'd finished the story. Wait a minute. It can't be the same story. Is it the story of what happened to Lotus? Is that why she disappeared- because she ran away with a Mongolian?"*

Startled by her train of thought Sammy shouted at Jerry and told him about her idea. He frowned; he didn't really remember the story. Sammy scowled at him and reminded him about what she had read in the museum.

"I think it's coincidence," he said. "I don't see how they can be about the same people."

Sammy was quiet. She didn't have any answers or real reason to think the stories were connected; just a strange feeling and the look Grandma had given her.

The professor and his students returned after lunch and everybody spent the afternoon together telling each other all the news from Beijing and hearing about the excitement of the festival backed up by lots of photos taken by David.

Life settled into the routine of daily digging once more. The children loved being around the students. David and Christine got on well with them too and enjoyed being able to assist them.

* * *

NEARLY TWO MORE WEEKS HAD PASSED AND JIA-LI and the children had finished in the temple and garden area. Jia-Li was going to move to another part of the site with the other students. Jerry and Sammy liked digging away from everybody else and asked if they could dig on the outskirts of the complex. Although the professor didn't think they would find anything he was happy to grant them permission as the children had proved themselves to be diligent and trustworthy.

Jerry and Sammy were often left on their own because Kim would wander off to look for Jia-Li but they didn't mind.

As the children removed the top layer of dirt from their chosen spot they struck an object. Using the brushes to carefully remove more soil they exposed a hair slide. It looked to be mainly intact with only a couple of broken teeth, although they couldn't be sure until it had been cleaned properly. It appeared to have a flower or something similar on the top as decoration. Jerry recorded all the relevant information on the sheet whilst Sammy took some photos. Then, carefully lifting it into a finds tray they took it to show Jia-Li who accompanied them to the finds tent so it could be cleaned and tagged.

"Are you sure you don't want to go?" asked Alan.

"No thank you. Tell the professor that with only a week left of our visit we don't want to miss any time here. We'll have a couple of days in Beijing before we return home," David assured them.

The students and Professor Cho were making another trip back to Beijing. Kim was going along, too, although he would be back on Saturday so he could take them to see his family as promised.

"Oh kids. Jia-Li says your hair slide is in the finds tent. She's not taking it back this trip because she's only just finished cleaning it. You're welcome to look at it whilst she's away but be extra careful. She thinks it might be of gold and jade which could make it valuable. She won't know for sure until she gets it back to the museum and does some more research." Kim waved as he got into the minibus.

David and Christine were just as eager as Sammy and Jerry to see the hair slide now that it had been cleaned up. It was exquisite. The comb was intact except for the missing teeth and the top appeared to be gold with a jade flower decorating it.

Sammy tried to contain the excitement that was welling inside her. "Can we stay here a minute longer?" she pleaded when her parents suggested returning the slide to its box and leaving.

"Okay, for five minutes but make sure you put it back properly so it's protected," said Christine.

Sammy waylaid Jerry.

"What?" he said when they were alone.

"Don't you see?" replied Sammy. "It's exactly the same as the hair slide Lotus was wearing."

"Not that again! You're imagining it," huffed Jerry.

Sammy gently rubbed the hair slide between her fingers so she could feel the texture of the flower. She started going hot and dizzy. She grabbed hold of Jerry. This time, even her legs felt wobbly. She opened her eyes and everything looked different.

9
Guards on the Great Wall

FOR A START SAMMY'S HAND WAS EMPTY. SHE WASN'T holding the hair slide anymore. The ruins and tents weren't visible. There seemed to be nothing around them except when they looked in the distance they thought they could see something; they looked like yurts.

Jerry had been staring open mouthed, swinging round in a circle.

"What's going on?" he said aghast.

"I don't know," said a frightened Sammy, her fingernails were now biting into Jerry's arm.

Jerry loosened her grip but kept hold of her hand.

"I'm scared. Where are the tents, and Mum and Dad?" asked Sammy.

"I don't know," replied Jerry. "Should we walk towards the yurts? Maybe Quan and Grandma can help us."

The mention of Grandma made Sammy start to think. It was as if all the cogs started whirring in her brain at once. Was this like the other dizzy spells? If so, why had the tents disappeared? What was different this time? She had been holding the hair slide. The slide that she thought belonged to Lotus. Sammy told Jerry all that she had been thinking; about the incidents at the terracotta warrior pit and museum being the same and how this felt similar just with a stranger outcome.

"So what are you saying?" asked Jerry bewildered as he stopped to face her.

"I don't know," said Sammy weakly.

"I know that voice. What are you really thinking?" demanded Jerry.

"Maybe we've gone back in time," Sammy blurted out. "It would explain why there are no tents. All my previous visions were of things in the past."

Jerry's face wore an incredulous look. "You have to be joking," he snorted.

Sammy hung her head. Jerry was probably right.

"Come on," said Jerry. "Let's see if we can find out what's going on."

It was beginning to get really dark. Stars were appearing in the sky, dotted about like specks of glitter. Luckily the moon was out, bathing the area in light or the children wouldn't have been able to see anything.

Suddenly they heard a noise; the repetitive thudding of something getting closer. The ground was beginning to vibrate and they could hear heavy breathing. A rider, leading a second mount, loomed out of the night. He caught sight of the children and slowed down. He looked Mongolian. He was wearing a long sleeved, dark blue robe and boots. Perhaps he was from Quan's tribe. He came to a halt beside Jerry.

"Hello my name is Temu and I'm from the Swan Tribe. I didn't realise anyone else was staying in the area," he said.

Jerry breathed a sigh of relief; just the person they needed! Sammy was more cautious. Surely everyone from Quan's tribe knew about the dig site. That same old feeling was nagging at her. Temu was obviously Mongolian but wasn't his robe slightly old fashioned? Not that she was an expert and the celebrations of the festival had meant that everybody had been dressed in their best. Even so...

"I could use your help," said Temu. "Can you come with me?"

"We'll be happy to help you because we need some help ourselves," replied Jerry.

"I'm heading to the wall. I have to meet someone there. Can you both ride together?" Temu gestured towards the spare horse.

Sammy looked at Jerry who nodded and gave her a boost up onto the horse before dragging himself up behind her; not very gracefully done but they were both on.

"We haven't done a lot of riding," he informed Temu, worried he was going to dash off at break neck speed.

"Don't worry. The horse is gentle. She will not let you fall. Hold onto the reins and each other and let her do the work," Temu reassured them as he handed them the reins.

They set off trotting to begin with but as all was going well they sped up to a slow gallop, (although that still felt fast to the two children who were more used to rambling horse rides). Jerry and Sammy were glad the evening was warm as the wind was now buffeting them, making them shiver.

"It's lucky I bumped into you. It will look less suspicious to any guards on the wall if we are travelling together than if I had been leading a spare horse," Temu explained.

"Guards!" exclaimed Jerry, shocked and confused.

Sammy kept quiet, but every nerve and muscle in her body seemed to have become alert.

"Don't be alarmed," said Temu. "There is rarely any trouble. Most of the soldiers stationed here are okay. They know our tribe is peaceful, living off the land and trading occasionally. We have no interest in China and leave them alone so they extend the same courtesy to us. I have managed to become good friends with one soldier called Cheng who will be on guard duty tonight at the main gate. We chose a night when he would be there because we thought it would make things easier."

Jerry's mind was beginning to scream in its confusion. All the talk of soldiers and conflict and guarding the wall didn't seem to make any sense.

Sammy was not slow to realise what Temu was talking about, but then she had been saying it from the start. "Told you so!" she hissed to Jerry behind her.

"What?" he asked, still floundering for an explanation.

Sammy rolled her eyes; he just didn't have enough imagination to conceive what had happened to them.

"We're nearing the wall," Temu interrupted their thoughts. "We'll go along it until we reach the outcrop of trees just before the gatehouse. Sammy, once we get there could you wait there with your horse?"

Sammy nodded. She was looking at everything in awe and wonder. It didn't look that different but the knowledge of what had happened changed her perception of what she was seeing.

10

Rescue & Realisation

TEMU, JERRY AND SAMMY RODE SILENTLY PAST the guards who were standing on the top of the wall, their spears in their hands. Somehow they appeared casual at the same time. Despite this, it didn't mean the small group wasn't being observed the whole time it was in sight. Maybe, as Temu said, the lack of threat made the guards more relaxed.

Jerry suddenly realised the wall looked different, but he couldn't say why, and there was no time to ponder about it— they had reached the trees. Everyone dismounted and Temu explained his plan.

"We've passed the guards without being challenged, which is excellent! Jerry, I want you to accompany me, on my horse, to the gate. Cheng should be there and we need to distract him so my friend can slip out unnoticed. She should make her way to you, Sammy, because she knows the horse will be here. You two should start back and Jerry and I will catch up with you."

As Jerry and Temu trotted out of sight, Sammy's heart started pounding in her chest with the fear of discovery or of something going wrong and the excitement and wonder of the situation into which she had been whisked. All these emotions crashed around inside her, making it impossible for her to stand still. However, when the horse stamped its hooves, it reminded Sammy that she wished to remain hidden, so she concentrated on calming her own nerves by stroking the mare which in turn quietened down. There she stayed, leaning against the side of the horse and gaining comfort from its soft hair, warmth and company. She was glad she wasn't there alone.

Temu and Jerry made their way along the length of the wall. The noise of the horse's hooves was muffled but still audible on the sandy ground. There were no more guards to be seen and it was whilst watching out for them that Jerry realised why the wall looked different. The wall now had a flat top; not the brick parapet he was used to from almost any image of the great wall he'd ever seen. He thought it odd but reasoned that some sections were in ruins while some had been rebuilt or repaired.

"We're almost there, Jerry," whispered Temu. We need to get ourselves into such a position that Cheng will be facing away from the gate. My friend, Lotus, can then slip through without being seen. The name Temu used gave Jerry a jolt. That was the name Sammy kept going on about, though perhaps it was a common name, belonging to an important flower in this area.

The sound of their horse stopping at the gate brought Cheng, the guard out. Cheng gave Temu a hearty welcome and he and Jerry smiled back at him, both feeling slightly guilty that they were about to trick him.

"A bit late to be out, isn't it? Surely you're not trading now?" he asked.

Temu laughed and deftly positioned his chestnut horse next to Cheng, partly blocking his view of the gate, whilst he and Jerry stood facing him so he had to look in their direction with the gate behind him.

"No. This is my cousin," he said indicating Jerry. "He's visiting with us before we leave on a trading journey. Unfortunately, being a bit excited, he was unable to sit still. I thought I'd bring him out for a ride to give him something to do and as I probably won't see you for a while I found myself riding this way."

"That's nice," said Cheng. "Any samples tucked away?"

"Funny you should say that," grinned Temu as he produced a small jade statue of a horse from his bag.

Cheng bent over to examine the statue and Temu was happy to let him have a closer look, especially as it stopped him noticing a slim figure moving past the horse and walking off in the opposite direction.

"How much for the statue?" inquired Cheng.

"You can have it," said Temu, starting to hand it over.

"I couldn't do that," Cheng protested. "Would your cousin like anything of mine in exchange?"

Jerry thought quickly, unsure of what to say. He didn't want to inadvertently insult Cheng. "Anything you are able to give me is fine. I'm happy to be learning how to trade and meet new people," replied Jerry.

"I don't have much on me whilst I'm on duty but I do have some money. Will that be enough?" said Cheng as he handed Jerry two round coins, each with a square hole in the centre.

Jerry smiled his thanks and added his goodbyes as Temu said that it was time for them to get back. He was distracted as he climbed onto the horse. These coins were old. They hadn't used money like this for a century or more. Realisation was beginning to creep in. Had Sammy been right all along? He'd thought Temu belonged to Quan's tribe but had he been talking about the ancient Swan Tribe? The storytellers had said they'd been around for centuries. Was this why there were guards on the wall? Had they really gone back in time and that far? Jerry felt a cold chill ripple through him. He wasn't sure of anything anymore. He needed to see Sammy and he needed some answers. He urged Temu to go faster.

11

The Truth About Lotus

THE SLIM CHINESE GIRL SQUEEZED THROUGH THE GAP SHE had made from opening the gate, advanced three steps and peered out, a wary look in her eyes. In front of her was the back of a soldier and making it slightly more absurd, the rear end of a horse. She could barely make out the silhouettes of two more figures just past the guard, which puzzled her, but she didn't have to time to dwell on it. She needed to get away before the guard turned round. She tiptoed past the back of the horse and carried on in the direction opposite to the group. She was talking to herself all the way, reminding herself to walk, not run, not to look back and to make it seem natural for her to be out walking at this time of night. She was nearly at the trees. She was sure that if anyone had been around, her heart would have given her away; it was hammering loudly against her chest. Then it missed a beat as a figure emerged from the trees. It was a girl!

The girl wore a surprised expression on her face as she called out quietly, "Lotus. Is that you?"

"How do you know me? What are you doing here?" the expression on Lotus' face gradually switched from amazement to terror.

"It's okay. I'm Sammy. Temu left me here with the horse. He wants us to start riding back together and he and my brother will catch up with us," Sammy told her.

Lotus made up her mind instantly, nodded to Sammy and motioned to her to climb onto the horse first. She arranged her finely embroidered pink silk dress so she too could climb onto the mare's back. Then, holding Sammy and the reins, they set off together at a walking pace.

Sammy didn't see any guards out on the wall and she was grateful for that. Her instinct was to turn round and look for signs of Temu and Jerry but she knew she shouldn't, so she strained for any sounds of their horse whilst dreading the sounds of anyone else approaching them. Luckily all was quiet as they headed away from the wall, back towards the open countryside.

The riders had both began to relax a little when the mare suddenly whinnied. To their amazement and fear, it was answered almost immediately. Then came the sound of horse hooves and the temptation became too much; they had to look over their shoulders.

"It's Temu!" shouted Lotus, joy evident in her voice.

Sammy realised they had been so caught up in trying to get away undetected that they been travelling in silence. Temu's horse drew level with them and everyone tried to dismount at once. With much bashing of limbs, the four were finally standing on the ground and Temu and Lotus were in each other's arms whilst Jerry and Sammy too shared a rare hug.

"We must keep going," said Temu. "We'll take you back to our meeting place and then Lotus and I must get back to camp," he continued, urging everyone back onto the horses once more. The creatures then sprang forward kicking up balls of dust as they fanned their long, tails.

As the group galloped off, Temu told Lotus about the part the children had played in the escape plan and Jerry and Sammy filled in any gaps in each other's stories. Temu told the children that he and Lotus would go to visit other friendly tribes with whom they traded for a while and rejoin the Swan Tribe once they were sure it was safe.

"Will Cheng get into trouble?" asked Jerry.

"If Lotus did manage to slip away unnoticed as planned, there should be no reason for anyone to get into trouble," replied Temu.

"He'll be fine," said Sammy with certainty.

"Shh!" whispered Jerry worried Sammy was about to let something slip.

They arrived at the spot where Temu had picked the children up and they all dismounted for the last time.

"We have to leave you now, unless there is anything we can do for you? You said you needed my help," Temu remembered.

Jerry gave Sammy a look, which spoke volumes. "No," he assured Temu. "We should be fine now," hoping as he said it that he was right.

"Thank you for all your help. No, keep them," Temu said as Jerry tried to give him the coins that Cheng had paid for the statue. "We are forever in your debt."

"Please accept this," said Lotus pulling a hairpin from her hair and giving it to Sammy. It was gold with a small, round jade bead at the end. Tendrils of her hair floated loose but she ignored them as she said her own goodbyes.

As Temu and Lotus climbed back onto the waiting horses, nobody noticed a hair slide fall out of Lotus' hair, finally coming to rest on the soil at their feet.

As Jerry and Sammy waved goodbye to the retreating figures they felt themselves going dizzy once more and as they gripped each other tightly they found themselves standing in the exact spot where they had found the hair slide which was now back in Sammy's hand. The children looked at each other then headed off in the direction in which they hoped would be the tents, their parents and their own time zone!

As the tents came into view, Sammy let out a slightly hysterical laugh, which was a mixture of relief, disbelief and happiness. "We'd better put the slide back and go to Mum and Dad. I don't know how we'll explain why we've been gone so long," confessed Jerry.

"Hello, you two. Did you put the slide back properly?" Mum checked as they came into the tent.

"Um. Yes," replied Sammy who could think of nothing else to say.

"What are you two going to do now? It's still early," remarked Dad.

Perplexed, Jerry glanced at his watch and was shocked to find that only twenty minutes had passed since they'd last seen their parents, which thankfully, saved him from having to come up with a believable lie!

"We're going to our tent. We'll probably turn in early. It's been a busy few weeks."

After kissing their parents goodnight, they turned and rapidly left the tent. They were in a hurry to be on their own.

12

More Questions than Answers

Jerry and Sammy flung themselves onto one of the sleeping bags and stared at each other in stunned silence.

"I can't believe what just happened. You were right all along," said Jerry finding his voice.

"I've got goose bumps," admitted Sammy. "Even though I was there, it feels unreal except I have this to prove it wasn't," she said holding the hairpin in the palm of her hand.

Jerry held out his coins. Both children's hands were shaking as they exchanged the gifts so that they could study them properly.

"What do we do with them? Do we have to give them to Professor Cho? Where do we say we got them?" asked Sammy. Everything seemed very complicated, especially as they hadn't processed everything they had been through yet.

Jerry thought hard, a frown settling on his face. "I don't think we have to give these to the professor," he said at last. "These were given to us when we went back in time. (It still feels very strange to say these words and mean them.) We didn't dig them up, so they don't belong to the university. They are rightfully ours. I'm not sure we can show them to anyone, though. Who would believe us?"

"You're right. It does sound bizarre doesn't it? How do you think it happened? Why didn't anyone notice we were wearing different clothes? Why could we understand what Temu and Lotus were saying?" The mention of Lotus halted Sammy's questions and brought a smile to her face. "Do you realise, we know the answer to the mystery laid out in the museum, but we can't really tell anyone about it?"

"I know. It's hard isn't it?" replied Jerry. "As for your other questions…"

Sammy looked sheepish.

"No, I wasn't having a go at you," Jerry assured her. "Those are the same questions I have buzzing around in my head. The main one has to be how or why it happened? Do you have any ideas?"

"Perhaps the hair slide is magical," suggested Sammy.

"Don't think so," mused Jerry shaking his head. "You were having visions before we found the slide, and Jia-Li touched it as well."

"True," agreed Sammy. "Well, if we can't answer that, how about, why we could all understand each other's language? Any theories?"

"No definite ideas. I can only assume that we looked and sounded how they would expect us to and we could understand each other through magic. If magic somehow transported us through time, then it must have enabled us to function in that time as well," reasoned Jerry.

Sammy had to stifle the impulse to laugh. Here was her sensible, technical brother having to use words like magic and rationalise how by this same magic they were transported back to another century. It sounded unreal to her and even though she usually was more imaginative, she could hardly comprehend the struggle that Jerry must have been having trying to make sense of it.

"You were brave, going off with Temu," admired Sammy.

Jerry smiled at the memory. "I'm not sure about that; no more than you staying behind on your own. It certainly was an incredible adventure, wasn't it? If it was your fault we were drawn into it— I'm glad." Jerry reached over and touched her hand affectionately.

"It was amazing!" she agreed. "I wouldn't have missed it for anything, however scary, but I'm really glad you were there!"

"I'd like to put all this down in my journal but I think the adventure has caught up with me. I'm so tired and my muscles are aching," yawned Jerry.

"There will be time to write in our journals in the morning before Kim gets back. I just want to sleep," mumbled Sammy, clambering into her sleeping bag without stopping to put her pyjamas on.

Jerry crawled into his sleeping area, closed the screen and scrambled into his sleeping bag fully clothed as well. He barely had time to turn out the light before Sammy was asleep so she missed his whispered 'goodnight'. He joined her in sleep with the very next breath.

* * *

SAMMY STARTED WRITING THE MINUTE BREAKFAST was over.

"What a cool time we've been having! Not only did we discover a beautiful hair slide, we were somehow whisked back through time to help rescue the girl who was wearing that hair slide. We'd read about her on our first day in China. So many things have happened that it's difficult to make sense of it, especially as we don't know how or why this happened. It was so brilliant to meet Lotus and Temu and to know through the museum and Grandma that they escaped and lived happily. Grandma— maybe there is someone we can talk to, though Jerry might not agree, I'll talk to him though. I wonder if he's right and if going back in time had anything to do with me. Why should I suddenly

have these visions and, if connected, how did the visions change from something I saw to us actually going back in time. I suppose I'll never know and should just enjoy the adventure. We are extremely lucky to have experienced what we have and I have the special gift from Lotus that I will treasure forever."

"Jerry, do you think that we could talk to Grandma about what happened to us? She believes in the truth of the story she recounts and she seemed to be saying things to me that would suggest an inkling of some sort."

"I don't know if we can trust her to keep our secret or even to believe us in the first place. It might be safer to just keep it to ourselves," replied Jerry finally. "I just don't know," he muttered as his pen started flying across the page again.

"What an adventure! After all the times I've started my journal with 'I travel back in time' it's now true-I've done it. I suppose I'll have to stop teasing Sammy about her vivid imagination, especially if it's because of her that we went back in time. I wonder if it was and how it happened. Maybe when I get home I'll do some research into time travel; see what I can find out. It was an amazing adventure; okay, not action packed but enough for me, especially when I realised that we were centuries away from where we should be without any knowledge of how to get home. Mind blowing! I'm glad Temu let me keep the coins. They will be my prized possession from now on."

"Children, Kim's here," shouted their mum.

They put their journals away and went outside to find not only Kim but Jia-Li as well.

13
The Wisdom of Grandma

KIM AND JIA-LI WERE BEHAVING RATHER SHYLY.
"I hope you don't mind Jia-Li joining us on our visit. I really wanted to introduce her to my family whilst we are all still in the same area," Kim said, an anxious look crossing his face as his eyes swept over everyone to see if he could gauge their reaction.

Jerry and Sammy went straight over to Jia-Li. After spending so much time digging in her company they were extremely fond of her and they had even tried learning some words in each other's language.

It was with mixed feelings that the Slades visited the Swan Tribe. Of course they were pleased to be seeing Kim's family again but they knew it would be for the last time. The dig site was being closed down on Monday and they were leaving China on Thursday.

Poppy was, as ever, ecstatic in her greeting and was pleased to make another friend. Quan and Grandma welcomed Jia-Li and she seemed to fit into the family comfortably. Sammy had noticed Kim and Jia-Li holding hands on the way over. She thought it was lovely and hoped everything went well for them.

Quan extended an invitation for everybody to join in with whatever they wanted to. Jerry asked if he could have a go at archery. The Mongolian bows had been developed specifically so that they could be used on horse back and looked like fun to try. He'd read how they used horns on the inside edges for strength whilst using sinew on the outside to enable them to stretch, thus making them strong enough to be developed into a shorter bow. Grandma forestalled Sammy's plans by asking her to sit with her for a minute. At this Sammy gave Jerry a pointed look, to which he shook his head. When she continued to stare at him, he shrugged his shoulders and left.

The minute they were alone Grandma said, "The ancestors walk with you."

Sammy's head shot up and she met Grandma's gaze. Thoughts were racing through her head. Did Grandma somehow know already? How did she start a conversation in which she confessed everything?

"Do you have something you wish to tell me?" said Grandma.

"How do you know everything?" questioned Sammy.

Grandma chuckled. "I don't know everything child. I feel aura and am sensitive to people's feelings. I believe the ancestors look after us and help us if we ask for help. You looked unsettled, like there was something on your mind. Then there was the unspoken conversation with your brother."

Sammy relaxed. The opportunity to tell was too great to resist. She told Grandma everything that had happened since they had arrived in China. It felt good to unburden herself at last.

"So Temu and Lotus galloped off and Jerry and I returned to the same spot where we'd uncovered the hair slide," she ended.

Sammy's face wore the same anxious expression that Kim's had earlier as she dared to raise her eyes to Grandma, unsure if she would be believed. Sammy's worries were unfounded. Grandma had tears glistening in her eyes and her face was filled with wonder and happiness.

"The story is true. I always knew it was. Now we even know their names. You are a very special girl," Grandma said clasping Sammy's hand.

"Why me?" asked Sammy. "Did I make this happen?"

"I don't know Sammy. It is a mystery why we are chosen to do things. What is important is that we keep ourselves open to the possibilities. Maybe that's why you succeeded where others have failed. Don't dwell on it. Enjoy your memories and live your life the way you want to, being true to yourself. And now, come let us join the others," said Grandma, rising from the bench.

Although Sammy still didn't understand the events that had taken place she felt better for having spoken to Grandma and left the yurt feeling happier.

The first people they saw were Kim and Jia-Li trying their hand at weaving. They were laughing at each other's results which did look a little funny. They were relaxed and having fun in each other's company.

"History repeating itself," suggested Grandma to Sammy, with a raised eyebrow.

"What a nice idea!" laughed Sammy.

14

Endings and Beliefs

SAMMY, ONCE AGAIN, TOOK ADVANTAGE OF THE PEACE and quiet in camp to update her journal before Professor Cho and the students returned.

"Grandma is an extraordinary woman. Her beliefs are entwined with her everyday life and even if there is no explanation for things she is happy to embrace them and believe in them. For whatever reason- I had flash backs and went back in time. I don't know how or why it happened or, even more scary, if it will ever happen again but I am going to be open to the possibility. Perhaps I needed to find something that belonged to Lotus to enable us to make the connection and to go back in time. Maybe my interest in the past and its people is as important as the here and now. I'm right to keep my other beliefs like fairies and unicorns no matter what anyone else might say."

When the rest of the students returned, the process of packing everything that wasn't necessary began at the camp. Professor Cho was in the finds tent with Jia-Li and Alan when Jerry and Sammy entered.

"The hair slide is beautiful," acknowledged Jia-Li to the children.

Sammy nudged Jerry.

"We were wondering, if it was at all possible, if um," Jerry was beginning to stammer.

"We wondered if this hair slide belonged to Lotus," said Sammy in a rush.

Professor Cho looked bemused but Jia-Li smiled. "I remember that story from the museum. I think this hair slide is like the one Lotus wears in the painting. I've always loved that story."

As the professor still seemed in the dark, Jia-Li filled him in on the story. Eventually he said, "There must have been many hair slides like this made. Even if it were the one that belonged to Lotus I can't see how it would have got all the way out here."

He smiled pleasantly at the children. The whole Slade family, their commitment and attitude to their work, impressed him. "I appreciate you telling me of your idea. If it did belong to Lotus the museum would probably need proof before putting it into that particular exhibition. However, I will mention it to Mr.Wu."

The whole family had enjoyed the dig experience but welcomed the comfort of the hotel showers and beds on their return. As they had got on well, David and Christine were going to try to arrange for Professor Cho to attend one of their digs in Britain. The children thought this was a good idea as the professor had treated them as part of the team and allowed them to gain vital experience.

Kim, Alan and Jia-Li arrived the next day to take the Slades out on their last trip together. They went to the Temple of Heaven. It was breathtaking and Sammy enjoyed the visit immensely. She had no visions but she was aware of an atmosphere and presence which she found comforting as she walked round, admiring the architecture and vibrant colours of the pillars and woodwork. She especially liked the carved marble panel depicting some dragons between the steps outside.

"I had a chance to look at the museum exhibit again," said Jia-Li. "I think the slide is the same as the one Lotus wears. I'm not sure we can ever prove it but I like to think that it is hers. I will let you know what they decide to do with it although it will be a little while before any of the finds are displayed."

Jerry and Sammy bid their new friends a tearful goodbye and promised to keep in touch.

The following day, after packing their bags for their return home next morning, Jerry and Sammy went to spend their last afternoon in the hotel garden. They took their journals with them.

The garden was as peaceful as Sammy had predicted and there was an air of serenity hanging over it. The scent of flowers wafted on the breeze and the trickle of water was relaxing.

Sammy's mind was in a romantic mood. *"The dig was everything I expected it to be and even better. I made great friends and had an unexpected and amazing adventure. Jia-Li believes that the hair slide belonged to Lotus. If she marries Kim and hears Grandma's story, will she connect the two and realise they are the same people? Maybe that's why Jerry and I had to go back, to keep the story alive for future generations. Temu and Lotus defied tradition by falling in love despite their different nationalities; Kim and Jia-Li are following in their footsteps. I hope they will be as happy."*

Jerry found the garden a tranquil balm to soothe his mixed up emotions. He was glad of the peace as he, too, put pen to paper. His journal entry was more philosophical.

"The dig was amazing, especially as we did our own work and recorded it. I definitely want to be an archaeologist someday. It's funny. We went to excavate a summer palace but I learnt more about Mongolian history, solved mystery centuries old, and saw what the Great Wall was like in its early stages of construction. I've learnt of many friendships across nationalities on this trip; Temu and Cheng, Temu and Lotus, Kim and Alan, Kim and Jia-Li and we too were welcomed by everyone. Aren't we lucky? So I finish this stage of my journal as I began...

*I'm the luckiest child alive. I travelled through time....
Who knows what tomorrow will bring?"*